90° *The Lick*

By La'mar Donald

*T*he Thomas's have come a long way from being convicted of murder on two seperate occassion's to being kidnapped, torchered and locked away in a metal health institution. Kenadi and Taven's diverse way of living has turned for the greater as they have now build and ventured off into the world of business and you can assure on this lick trouble is yet to arise as detective

Jackson who also is battle between his new found love and finding the two agents that went against the grain. Will they come to a conclusion.
Stay tuned..

LLC.

90° The Lick© 2021 by La'mar Donald

Artwork by CHOPPTRIGG@ Element Of Design

"You already know what time it is..."

Thanks for the support Authoress Kiesha Michelle

One
Kenadi

"*A*fter our wedding and seven day honeymoon, I was exhausted and still in disbelief but the excitement still remained.

I had actually married the man of my dreams and due in July with not one but two babies and every since I broke the news to Taven about the pregnancy he's monitored my every move setting limits on everything I do."

We returned home to a forty two foot Sailfish boat for Taven and a brand new sleek and sexy Rose red Porsche Panamera for me and from the looks of things before long we would soon have a car lot.

I thought about my future as I got up to fix myself a grilled ham and cheese sandwich with Dill pickle Lay's potatoe chips and of course my favorite Lemon water and honey.

Let me guess being pregnant had a lot to do with these crazy cravings that I had obtained and according to the gynecologist I was sixteen weeks and every thing was looked perfect and to the public's eye I was nearly showing and not only could I feel the babies growing as time weren't by I watched as my belly got bigger and rounder. I made my way to the kitchen and the dogs were no where in sign but I knew they were some where close by, very close.

Sheena and Vina were in the living room near the front door, Nina was by Tue double sliding doors gnawing on a chew toy.

When we left for the wedding I took Sheena and Nina to my man Retro Active for a little training and I'll admit he had done a damnd good job, they were always on point.

I had a day ahead of me and my schedule was looking like my belly, full!

First thing first was to call Angiana Hall, the realtor in Oregon about the condo and in two days Taven and I were going out West. We found a nice little castle off Coos Bay just off the coast line which was Taven idea and I refused to argue or put up a fight because he did have a boat.

I though about my cousin Deyun who's plane landed at eight tonight and I knew it was now or never and mandatory that we met up and discussed the lick on the building and decide on on the business and perfect location and cost.

I waited for my lemon water to boiling mean while I told Alexa to dial his number but it went directly to his voicemail then it hit me, it was nine a.m. and knowing him he was probably just now going to sleep. My only option was to leave a message, he'd be calling before I knew it.

I sat at the round silver and black glass table and couldn't help but think about Taven who had flown to Oregon to work on getting a permit for a landing pad built near the house. The helicopter was a wedding gift along with twins.

I almost forgot that I had to order appliances for our new crib and make sure everything was delivered to the right place and last but not least "Totally Envogue" my ever so successful nail and hair salon which was really doing numbers."

I dialed Angiana's number and on the second ring she picked up.
Before I could I ask any question's she was already giving me the run down on what I wanted to know and from the sound of things shit was looking good, real good."

The Tudor style mid century structure of the condo really caught my eye and had a beautiful view of the ocean.

The high gables and dormed windows were perfect it was a beautiful sight at night and produced just the right amount of light in the day.

She said, "We are actually laying the finishing touches and in the morning and in the morning we'll do a quick run through and make sure everything is everything then it's all on you."

I thanked her and assured her that I would see her in a day or so.
We hung up and I called Lexi

to booked my flight but her
line was busy as usual.
I then took a shower a hot
shower and got dressed
letting my hair air dry which
would naturally create a lot
of kinky curls.

Then to make things worse it
took me five minutes to get
my juicey ass in my Ralph
Lauren jeans and another
five to find a shirt.
Finally I decided on a
stripped purple and yellow
Polo shirt along with a pair of
white air force ones. My cute
days we done for now I was
more focused on being
comfortable. I applied just a
touch of eye liner and as I
looked in the mirror my cell
phone vibrated. I wasn't a bit
surprised, it was Deyun

returning my call.

He said, "Kenadi cousin what it do, open up I'm out front!"

I made my way to the front door and opened and before he could get in the house good he said , "The building is located in a plaza off Slider Rd. amongst various business's. "

He began to name a few and what I had in mind fit perfectly. I was banking on a restaurant serving Bourban chicken, an assortment of rices, sauteed veggies and salads. Deyune face lit up and I could hear the excitement in his voice.

He said, "That sounds nice, that way the employee's that work in the plaza want have far to go get a decent meal and what do you think about selling a little liguor in the evening?"

"I'm cool with all that, add that up too," I replied but what surprised me was when he told me not to worry about the building, that he had all of that covered. What I call a fifty-fifty deal and from the looks of things Deyun had wised up a little bit and I was anxious to find out.

He settled at the table and said, "How soon do you think you can fly up and check things out?"

"We leave for Oregon in two days, I say let me get things situated and we'll be up by the end of the week.

 Then before I could get out another word he said, "Kenadi cousin do you have any work?"

I thought to myself, "Oh hell here we go," but I knew he was good for it I just needed to know what was really going on.

I said, "I'm always good, what the lick read?"

"The FED's picked up my supplier on conspiracy to distribute drugs and trafficking from state to state and according to the streets he's facing about thirty in a Federal facility and me personally I'm not about to take any chances plus I refuse to open up any new doors therefore I want have to close any plus I need a way."

I couldn't deny him as I asked what he had in mind.

"He said, "I need ten pounds, I got twenty thousand in cash like right now and I know you got that gas!"

I moved quick as I shot up the stairs failing to realize that I was carrying a small load. I went into my closet and pulled out the extra ten pounds I'd put back.

By the time I'd made it back down stairs he had returned with a Bottega Veneta back pack and we began counting doing business

He sarcastically said, "Kenadi there's and extra hundred in there for you tho grow on."

I couldn't help but laugh as I ran the dead guy's through the machine. All was well as I then began to place the marijuana in black trash bags. He knew every thing would weigh up.

I wanted to ask how he planned on getting all of this back to Kentucky but Deyun was like that monkey off "Lion King" Rafiki, he knew

the way.
He then condratulated me again and thanked me for cruise and good time he'd had and the next thing I knew he was on his way.

I gathered my McM bag and place the twenty thousand in the safe. I then spent another five minutes digging in my bag looking for the remote to the Panamera before finally making my way to the garage.

Before I backed out I called Lexi and told her to book a flight for two and that I needed to be on the next thing smoking.
She assured me that she had it and would call me back and let me know the exact time.

After about fifteen minutes of riding I pulled into the parking lot of the salon and couldn't find a place to park.

Camillia Japonica was at the front desk booking appointments and was relieved when she saw me walk the double glass doors. She got up handing me the cordless phone stating that she needed a break.

I looked at the log sheet and to my amazement there were over fifty appointments today alone, I couldn't help but smile cause lately all I'd been seeing was dollar signs.

Camillia Japonica asked was I hungry because she was starving. I wasn't all that hungry but I did have a taste for a Chilli cheese Frito steak wrap, so we agreed on going to the Lettuce patch deli that way if i got that craving I could order all the pickles I wanted.

I left Jy-Jy in charge while we stepped out and I let Camillia drive.
She talked about how nice the wedding was, about some guy that she had met and how much she enjoyed the cruise.

As we pulled into the deli my cellphone vibrated. I glanced at the screen and it was my hubby calling.

I answered and before I could get out a word he said, "How are you and my babies and what are you doing."

"We are okay just missing you and I'm at the Lettuce patch deli with Camillia, how did the permit go?"

"They are really giving a brother a hard time but you know like I know, bands will make them dance."

"I laughed because hecould be really sarcastic and funny at times."

 I said, "Deyun came by this morning and apparently he has found a place in the plaza not far from where he's staying and for a decent price and surprisingly he said that he had all of that covered. We are going to try the restaurant thing and see how it works out, I'm thinking Bourbon, Teriyaki and curry chicken, a variety of rices, sauteed vegetables and salads. I want to call it Raven's Haven."

Taven wasted no time and didn't think twice about it.

He said, "Love this is your world I'm just in it, whatever you want to do I'm down with the lick."

That was one thing I loved about him, what ever I wanted he made sure I got it and had no problem going to

get it or making it happen.
I also explained to him what the realtor had said and that I might fly up a day early and all I was waiting on was Lexi to let me know what time my flight leaves.

He said, "Just let me know so I can meet you at the airport."

I told him that I love him and that I would talk to him later and we hung up.

For the most part my day seemed akwardly perfect and things were going as planned. Camillia Japonica studied the menu and asked what I wanted to eat.
I replied, "Pickles."
That's all I had a taste for.
She ordered a Chilli chess

foot long hot dog with the works, bannana peppers, relish, mayo, and extra cheese along with a two Baja Mountain Dew's and my pickle.

I had to ask how she maintained that shape with her eating habits.

She replied, "Good sex and a membership at the gym."

We both couldn't help but laugh at her statement which was probably all but true. I then told her that I was leaving for Oregon maybe a day early and it was on her and the crew to hold things down.

She said, "That want be a

problem and nothing new, we been doing that."

That I couldn't refute, she was stating all facts and I had to admit they'd done an excellent job.

Thirty minutes later we were back at the salon and the customers seemed to flow in with the rhythm of the day.

I made sure every one was okay before I went and sat in the car contemplating on all I had to do before I left town.

I dialed my dad's number and he answered on the first ring.

He said, "Hey baby doll how are you and where is my son-in-law?"

"I'm good and Taven is in Oregon. They have finished the renovating a day early and he's seeing the people about building a heli pad, why what's up?"

"Nothing I was just wondering where my boy was at."

"Where is my mother matter fact ask her would she like to fly to Oregon with me, I'm going to need her help."

A second later I heard him call her name and before I knew it she was on the line.

She said, "Hello my dear child how are you and them little lives growing inside of you?"

"We are all fine. I was wondering would you like to fly with to Oregon, I'm going to need some help arranging somethings?"

"Sure when and what time are we leaving?"

I told her that I was still waiting on Lexi but to go ahead and pack up and be ready hopefully in the morning.

Two
Taven

I hadn't been in Oregon forty eight hours and I was already enjoying the new atmosphere.

Kenadi had an aunt and uncle that lived a few blocks away.

Her uncle known to many as Boo-Boo was her father's brother, the true definition of a player and natural bone hustle.
He owned a strip club and a restaurant aloing with his ace coon boon who went by the

name Goldie which was his rght hand and wife's brother.

Twanna and Goldie were born with silver spoons in their mouths. Their great grandfather had established a funeral home and became well known and labled the best at what he did.

Boo-Boo on the other hand knew people who knew people that knew a few more people on top of them people and after he' d finally got the permit approved for he said, "It's all about who you knew and how you conducted yourself.

Thirty minutes later we pulled up to what looked like a miniature castle. We drove up the stone drive way to the entrance and before we came to a complete stop two Doberman's and a pit bull were pacing back and forth around the blue sapphire BMW X2.

As Boo-Boo put the SUV in park I said, "Ain't no way I'm going to get out with them retards lurking around."

I wasn't scared I just didn't want take a change at getiing bitten. I was strapped and my trigger finger was itching for some attention.

Boo-Boo rolled down the window and said, "Yeild til I spark" and the three dogs disappeared around the house.

 Unk had a dumb lingo. We got out and made our way to the front door where we were greeted by his wife.

She didn't look a day over Forty and was hotter than a desert. She had jet black hair that was pulled back in a pony tail. She also stood around five seven with silky dark chocolate skin and I couldn't help but notice his thick she was in her legging stretch pants.
She had all the features off an ex-stripper.

She said, "Hello."

I introduced myself and followed Uncle Boo-Boo into

the luxurious living quarters but before I could take a seat he said, "What would you like to drink as he made his way to the mini which contained all of the top shelf drinks known to an alchoholic but I wasn't really in the mood for a drink so I just told him to give me what ever he was drinking.

He walked over to a miniature wood grained fridge and pulled out two green bottles of Dos Equis a drink that I've never had.

He said, "This here nephew is a gentlemen's beer, drink up and don't get to comfortable or tied up because tonight we are going to Rilynn's."

"What's that?"

He said, "Hold on a second"
as he walked up the stairs.

I sat back on the charcoal
gray love seat and listened to
Curtis Mayfield, drifting as I
let the music take me away.
Just as I finished my second
bottle aunt Twanna asked
was I hungry. I was then I
wasn't.

I said, "Do you have any
mangoes?"

She gave me this crazy look
and said, "Nope, just
blueberries and cherries
Florida boy."
I shook my head and told her
I was good and began to

texting Kenadi.
"What time does your plane land?"

"Nine a.m."

"Okay I'll call you shortly and I love you."

"It's the same!"

I loved that women, I had literally molded her into a female version of myself.

I could hear uncle Boo-Boo up stairs having a faint conversation along with an unfamiliar voice.

I looked around into the kitchen and aunt Twanna was still doing her thing with the pots and pans therefore I knew it wasn't her and had no clue as to who it could've been.

Moments later Boo-Boo came back down stairs and said, "Nephew let me introduce you to my daughter Drica, Drica this is Taven, your cousin's Kenadi husband.

She scanned me from head to toe and said, "Nice, what's up cousin?"

I loved my wife to death and I wasn't going for nothing strange but the little lady was tight in all the right places and then the crazy thing about it was she was damn near identical to Kenadi.

She had light brown eye's complimented by her skin

tone and wore her hair in a bun. She stood around five six and the cat suit that she wore was tighter than the skin on a pomegranate.

Before she left she gave me that look and said, "Get my number from daddy and call me if you need anything."

I thought to myself, "Damn" as I watched her walk away, unk broke me out of that trance.

He said, "Drica, that's my girl, this is her last year at Oregon state, she finally getting that degree in forensics. I think lab technician and my grandson K.K. will be here soon, really any moment and what ever you do don't let that kid get you out if your element, he's just like Drica. All gas no breaks.

"I'll be back shortly Goldie and I got a drizop on a few of them thizang's, get some rest and be ready by nine."

"I replied, "Bet and before I knew it I was in a deep sleep dreaming about the love of my life and everything that came with it.

Around eight thirty I was awakened by light taps on my feet. I look at my Louie V Tambour horizon watch then at Boo-Boo.
He said, "Nephew get on up and get your shit together, our night starts in thirty minutes.

I got up and retrieved my
bag from the rental car.
Before I took my shower I
found aunt Twanna in the
living room with the three
dogs and said, "How should I
dress for tonight.

She looked me from head to
toe and said, "Florida boy just
do you."

I opened the bag an grabbed
the first outfit I saw which
was a gray, violet and white
Balmain polo shirt and a pair
of gray Balmain slacks.
At nine on the head we were
out the door and I'll admit
unk looked nice.
He wore a navy blue and
white button up, a pair of
white slacks and a navy blue

blazer all by Donna Karen.

As we made four way to the garage I noticed that he had more cars than a little bit. He pressed a button on a remote and a forest green King Rancher came to life. We hopped in and was on our way to Rilynn's.

Little did I know and come to find out Rilynn's was a strip club, top notch to be exact that sat on the corner of Simmons and Roxie Dr. and as we pulled into the parking lot I couldn't he'll but notice how long the lines were. Once we were on the inside unk pointed in the direction of the bar where a group of females were located but it was hard to make out who they were through the smoke. As we approached the bar I noticed that there were a number of NBA stars in the building.

I said, "Unk this place is bumping" then what surprised me most was when I spotted Serena, Venus and Layla Ali heading to V.I.P.

Thought to myself, "Unk most definitley got it going on. Shortly after I met with Goldie and we all made our way to the second floor and it was even nicer.
Rilynn's had a total of sixty five strippers, twenty on each floor and the other five women were the show stoppers.

We bee lined through the crowd making our way to the bar where I ordered Remi V on the rocks and by the time I'd starred on my second cup the place had gotten all the way live and I was enjoying every moment.

<u>Three</u>
Traffic in The Sky

*T*ime had passed and I had accomplished more than expected. My cell vibrated and with a text from Lexi.

It read: Your plane leaves at seven and don't miss your flight...
             XOXOXOXO

For a split second the things that had occurred two years ago flashed in my mind but I drowned that with thought of how much I had gained and advanced from it. I never thought in a million years that I would've went through the trials and tribulation I'd endured and be where I am til this day.

You know the bible say's that god want put no more on you than you could bear and I was a living testimony.

Unbelievably I had accomplished a alot in no time. I had the salon, the super yatch, my hubby, the twins and a restaurant in the making and I wasn't going for nothing strange, this part three you suppose to know what the lick read!

I text my mom letting her know what time to be ready

then I packed my bags and got settled for the evening with Mr. Taven Thomas a.k.a Three on my mind.
My belly seemed to be getting bigger by the day and honestly being a mother never crossed my mind and I must admit I was super excited about everything.

I told myself that this was the begining and before I left I recorded everything aunt La'raine needed to know on Alexa and for some odd reason she'd been missing in action then I just figured she was out with a male friend and left it at that.

The following morning I got up around five forty and text mom letting her know that I would be over in thirty minutes. Roughly at six fifty we were at terminal twenty three with our luggage aboarding our flight on our way to Oregon.

The flight was just over an hour long and by the time we landed at Coos Bay private airport I was exhausted and not in the mood as I took my cellphone out of my text Taven.
He met us at terminal twelve and by the time our luggage came around Taven approached excitedly to see us. He hugged me rubbed my belly and greeted mom and said, Baby I miss you"

followed a big sloppy kiss, all tounge.

My mother stood there looking crazy.
She said, "Well damn Taven just suck her whole face off, there ain't that much love in the world."

I replied, "Yes it is!"
I then text the realtor letting her know that I bae arrived a day early.
She text back that she would be ready when ever I was.

Oregon was a beautiful site and humid as hell. Thirty minutes later we were driving up a pebble driveway to our new estate.
 I was excited and couldn't wait to see the renovations.

As we made up to the double glass door we were greeted by Angianna and another female realtor.
We all introduced ourselves and began our tour and I'll be honest I was loving every square inch but I couldn't help but notice how the other realtor kept eyeing Taven.
 I quickly called her to the side and let her know that he was taken, mine meaning bolonging to me and that she better get her mind right before I pushed what she was thinking to the left.
 I'll admit she was a little cutie who made gone of the ugliest faces ever but she didn't say a word.

An hour later we'd covered every square inch of the crib and I was impressed at what we had done.
Ma was ready to lay her touches in the kitchen and other nursery for the twins. I called and made sure that the people at the furniture place had the right address then we're all went out to eat at uncle Boo-Boo's restaurant called "Off the flames."

There were hibachi grill located in the center of each table equip with a venting system that pulled the fumes through subterranean air ducts and every person that worked up front did the cooking.

 They all moved about from station to station rotating adding their touch to each meal.
They all had a specialty so there was no way to decipher out which cook was the best and the most exciting part was watching it all take place.

The color scheme was brilliant. The hostess wore Sphere blue blazers and the servers wore Orion blue butchers aprons and ear pieces like the secret services for communications which I thought was really cool.

We all studied the menu and came to an agreement on marinated roe and bacon,

Carolina golden rice, teriyaki tuna burgers and sauteed vegetables. I myself on the other hand order a mango salad along with sliced pickles.
As we ate we discussed future plans along with investments and before we knew it time had caught up with us.

We were almost late meeting with the delivery people and on our way back to the crib I contacted aunt Twanna to see if she wanted to help, she agreed but had to wait til Drica arrived.

The last time I had them was twelve years ago and I was dying to see my cousin.

Growing up we had always

been mistaken for sisters and if there was ever a such thing as twin cousins then that's just what we were with way to much in common.
We even shared the same taste in men.
 Taven had that young Bob Marley look especially with dreads and Haitian Rabbi, Drica's man favored Kymani Marley.

Taven would never know but I thought he was kind of cute and I knew if she'd met Taven then she was thinking the same thing but Taven had nothing to worry about because I belonged to him and only him.

Four
The Odds

*D*etective Jackson arrived at the Citrus building a little after nine a.m. and wasn't expecting what awaited him. Before he left for his much needed vacation he had more cases that he could handle but his main focus was finding Slovene' and Easom.

He sat on the edge of the office chair with his elbow on his knee along with his chin in his hand staring at the three manilla envelopes crammed with material adding to the scattered papers that were already pilled on his desk.

Cheif Sadirolf in Pensacola had tried to contact him days prior leaving a message with Margret for him to get in contact while he was on the cruise.

He knew he didn't have time to waste but the getaway was much needed plus he enjoyed the time that he and Roseacia had spent together.

The day after, another detective in Pensacola had called, Slovene' had been spotted in two different locations.
A couple had seen his picture on the six o'clock news and instantly recognized him in Destin Florida at a Circle K then hours before hurricane Travis hit Panama city he was

seen in the parking lot of a local hardware store and by the time the owner put two and two together he was long gone, swept away with the heavy winds of the malicious weather.

Finding the two ex-agents wasn't the only problem that the Citrus building had gained. There was a new detective in town who was certified in two fields to many.

Her name was Sariya Nazira and she'd recently transferred from Orlando Florida.

Back in Orlando she was Sergeant over the drug unit and apart of the Drug enforcement administration.

Out of the thirteen years in the field six of them she played detective in the homicide unit and did a helluva job.

Sariya was born in Trinidad and at the age twelve her parents migrated to the U.S. relocating in Valdosta Georgia. At an early age she was introduced to this line of work through both parents.

Sa'riya was six feet even and amazingly beautiful with a body of a goddess, fiestier than a cornered cat with a temper equivalent to a jar of tamales.
Sergeant Kimberly wasted no time as he introduced the two.

At first Jackson was at a loss for words as he admired her beauty. She had a caramel latte skin tone along with features of young Rosie Perez.

Jackson knew by her attitude and looks that she was going to be a bit of a problem. Jackson introduced himself and told her to take a seat as he handed her a Manilla envelope that contained the profiles of two drug runners that were wanted for trafficking and a tripple homicide that had occurred on Palmetto Ave.

He began explaining what leads he had and who the two men were running for but she protested asking about

Slovene' and Easom and she demanded to know every detail the case and the men.

An hour later Jackson had given her the run down plus the extra's and he couldn't help but see the determination that she had.

As she gathered the files and began to leave Jackson said, "What about the trafficking and triple homicide?"

She stopped momentarily and said, "Just chill I got this" as she left headed in the direction of her office.

Sergeant Kimberly and Murphy made their way into the office to discuss the latest and how they planned on finding Slovene' and Easom and as of the two men had a touch down with a late lead and from the way things were looking they weren't about to catch up.

Jackson read over the report that the officers over in Pensacola had faxed and even Ray Charles could see that they were a few steps behind the men.

Question was how did he manage to get out of the hand cuffs and shackles killing the two transportation officers and according to the report both officers throats were slit with an unidentified object with precise precission. The officer that sat in the back with Slovene' was the first to die then the driver who lost control of the cruiser crashing into multiple vehicles before wrapping the vehicle around a pole.

Now the question remained about his where about and where he could be headed. They had no idea what he had up his sleeve, armed or not he was dangerous and a menace to society.

Little did they know he had passed through a number of states on his way to Rhobe Island killing five more people along the way.

In Rhode Island their was an apartment that was being used as a safe house containing valuable information that left a trail. Being smart and dangerous was a deadly combination.

Slovene' had attended a military camp in Brazil where he graduated then enlisted in their special forces.

After five years and a honorary discharge he made his way to Bolivia where he hooked up with an old friend who was dating Byron Flekk also known as Don Easom.

Easom was a hired hand whole traveled back and forth from South America to America who got paid a pretty penny for his work. Through multiple drug deals with Panther, Tyga Ransom's youngest brother he was hired to kill Trayven Thomas and by this time he had a life saving saved in a bank over seas.

It took many years to accomplish the task but to no avail it was done.
The two men moved to Tallahassee with clean records along with the proper credential's, passed all of the exams and before they knew it they were on the force with the mission at hand.
Fourteen years later the chance finally presented its self and was finalized.
Detective Robinson wasn't suppose to die and Jackson promised himself himself that the two would pay, he put that on everything and

some.
He thought about the two men and no one gave any thought or had any suspicion of the two. They carried themselves accordingly and played their roles to a tee.

<u>Five</u>
In Rotation

*K*enadi had spent fifty thousand in renovations which wasn't bad. Another plus was that it had a beach front in the perfect location a few minutes away from Taven's boat.

 The launch pad for his whirly bird was also under construction and the condo was now fully furnished with everything new, the hard part was arranging everything.

The kitchen was equip with a glass top stove, double oven and side by side fridge. All stainless steel. The lox sultan

tile design was gray, black and white in color.
The twelve by eight shark tank sat on an island in the kitchen and contained a number of exotic life from the deep blue sea.

The walnut and blackened steel entry wall complemented the adjacent painted panels walls which out lined the European kitchen cabinets.

The Silestone counter top matched the painted beams and the breakfast area had French Louis XV chairs covered in white suede which encircled the granite table top.
The grand reception room had high ceilings loaded with

expensive lighting fixtures and each walls contained an exclusive painting that set the tone.
The custom fire place and glass sliding door panels opened to a covered deck.

Kenadi surprised Taven with a giant in home theatre and a mini gym that was located in the full size basement. They also had a four car garage and plenty parking space.

Shit was really groovey like on some Austin Powers shit.

While Kenadi and the family helped the interior designer put things together they updated one and another on their life and differences.

Mean while Taven and Haitian Rabbi plotted on a million dollar investment in stocks down in the basement.

Biotic botony was new to Taven and he hadn't never heard of the Florida based firm that produced funding for real estate such as green houses and medical labs.

Haitian Rabbi gave him them the run down and at the same time he calculated how much they would invest.

Thirty one states had already legalized marijuana and the people in Washington D.C. had legalized it for medical and recreational uses. They calculated the people that smoked medical and none medical marijuana and according to the analytics over eight point six billion dollars was made and it was going up by twenty five percent.

Rabbi had a very close friend from Canada, home of the most pot ever stocked and medical marijuana grower who lived in California licensed to grow and sale. Her name was Pomikii Propane and after discussing their investment Rabbi contacted Rabbi and set up a meeting so she could break down how a strain was created along with the stocks in real estate funding firm Biotic Botony.
Mean while the four ladies reminisced and made plans

for the twins, discussed money along with the rights of a female.

The designing of the shark tank was tricky because everything looked beautiful.

The three week old nurse shark was a brownish white specimen and wasn't very big in size. The coral reefs came in eleven illuminescent colors that gleamed even brighter under the black lights.
The sea aninome along with the sea squirts floated in place as they adjusted to their new environment along with the star fish, algae eater and sea horse.
There was more exotic life than one could name and an amazing site to see.

Around eleven p.m. everyone had became tired and exhausted. Majority of the heavy lifting had been done so that was a plus now all Kenadi had to do was book their flight for Kentucky and after a long sucessful day Taven and Kenadi had finally had some time to enjoy on be and another.

Every day she was getting closer and closer to her due date and as the days went by she could gradually feel and see her body transforming.

Before long she was going to have to lay down her hustle until she gave birth.

Taven and Haitian Rabbi had a flight to catch in the morning to California on some business while Krystina and Kenadi had a one way flight to Kentucky, shit was really in rotation.

<u>Six</u>
Another Dose

*C*heif Jackson day was a doozy and the time had came for him to settle and have a drink but that plan was delayed due to a phone call which led to two more unexpected call.

Margaret had took the call and informed him that he had Alaska Jade Robinson, Detective Robinson's daughter was on line one.

The call was urgent and she really needed to talk to the chief.

He picked up the phone and hit line one.

She said, "Chief sorry to bother you but I'm down in Miami and I have a detective here that knows this Easom, Byron Flekk and there's reason to believe that Easom is in South America and Jaxson Slovene' could be on his way and here's the lick."

"Another officer did a routine traffic stop on a turquoise Audi A4 that was speeding, I'm talking eighty in a fifty zone then come to find out the driver is the wife of the Easom workers. Apparently your ex agent has been dealing drugs for a very long time. The young lady goes by the name of Katiesa Manning. She had a suitcase full of

China White and sixty thousand in cash and she was booked and charged she did eventually get a bond but for one reason and one reason only and you of all people should know how the cookies crumble also the detectives here in Miami buttered the little duck and boy did she quack. Now we are hoping she gives some type of lead to who ever the brains of the operation are and we do have surveillance from Perrine to South beach and eventually she'll give us what we are looking for.

She also has a husband by the name of Prentice Manning who has a clean record and all she is saying everything belongs to the men her husband works for and she

did was follow an order.
As of now we haven't been able to locate him but I'm pretty sure he'll show up before long."

"The chief applied a little to much pressure over in the drug squad and according to her, there's a safe house in Rhode Island where they'be been manufacturing drugs and holding large quantities of money. I'm only letting you know because there's a price that somebody is about to pay for my fathers death and all I'm saying is you all better get to them before I do."

Jackson was amazed at the information he'd just received and as she talked, he wrote documenting the facts

and this was just what they needed.
He assured her that he was on the job and that justice would be served. He vowed to contact her as soon as something new came his way.

Detective Jackson powered down his laptop, locked his office and made his way to the parking lot. He really needed to clear his mind and he knew just what to do.

He paired his cellphone to the bluetooth and called Rosecia. He knew shyte could get the information that he needed plus they hadn't talked all day long and he was really missing her.

Before they left four the wedding they had already begun building a relationship and the feelings that they shared were mutual.

Jackson was finally feeling alive and deeply in love. Rosecia wasted no time as she answered in the first ring.

"Hey babe, how was your day?"

"The usual case after case, you know and how has your day been?"

"Nothing out of the ordinary, a meeting here another one there. The stocks in oil has sky rocketed, an all time high and today we had a meeting about it. I'm trying to talk a few of my employee's out of doing the unthinkable. They think investing will bring billions which is true but whose to say that the stock want plummit next week. They lose a cool million or two then be looking crazy bat me crazy like its my fault, I know I've seen it one time to many."

"Before Grandfather Valez struck with the Black gold he lost a lot of money, now I'm stuck with a small mess and I don't want to put my foot in my mouth."

Jackson laughed and said, "You can put your foot in my mouth if you would like."

Roseacia couldn't help but smile and laugh, then out of nowhere he surprised her and said, "I love you!"

Silence lingered momentarily before she broke it. She said, "I love you too."

Rosecia then asked what his plans were for the weekend.

He hadn't recall thought much about it and it really didn't matter as long as he didn't miss the Dolphins game on Sunday.

He said, "I haven't made plans yet and the Thomas case has been closed but the agents are still at large and I want rest until the two are in custody along with everyone who played a role pays up and what the odds of there being a safe house located in Rhode island?"

"Honestly I don't know but I wouldn't doubt, Tyga Ransom and his brothers were all living in Rhode Island. And to my knowledge they still are. Maybe you should try contacting one of them and see what you can find out."

Tomorrow I have to go to the exotic import, the brakes on the X 30i locked and I've spent to much money to be having these kind of problems and I hate to run but I need to get with my father and go over these charts and I'll call you back shortly.

"I'll be waiting, "Love You."

Rosecia replied, "It's the same!"

As he drove alone he made up his mind and went to the Seminole Lounge.

The Hawks were playing the Mavericks, a game that he didn't want to miss.

He tried to focus and clear his mind of everything but he couldn't pass up the joy that she brought into his life. She made him feel twenty years younger but the position that he held at the Citrus building made him feel the opposite.

His next objective was to find a contact in Rhode Island and his secretary was the on be for the job.

Inside of the lounge he found the perfect seat located directly in front of one of the many Eighty inch plasmas that hung from the wall.

He ordered Tangueray No.5 on the rocks for starter's along with ranch dressing and a twenty four piece Hawaiian mild wings.

The gentleman that sat next to him asked who did he like.

He said, "I like number seventy two, Luna Doncic'. I'll bet three hundred dollars that he scores over thirty

points."
The wasted no time as they shook hands sealing the bet.

Around and ten p.m. the game had ended and Luke had put up a total of thirty eight points.

The guy handed Jackson three crisp hundred dollar bills and told him good game just as he got up to leave.

Jackson paid his tab and exited the bar making his way to the parking lot.

He pulled out into the two lane traffic followed by an orange and white Harley Davidson truck who trailed him for at least four blocks.

<u>Seven</u>
Raven's Haven

Kenadi and Krystina boarded their flight to Kentucky and all Kenadi could think about was her new business venture.
The seven forty seven landed at Kentucky international airport. As the exited the terminal and went for their luggage Kenadi texted Deyun their location. Moments later they met up and he welcomed them to the "The blue grass state."
As they approached a metallic blue E- class

Mercedes Benz Kenadi was already liking the place.
Deyun used a remote to open the trunk, the doors unlocked and the classy car came to life.
The ladies looked at one another in surprise.

Krystina said, "Well damn, somebody doing good."

Deyun couldn't do nothing but laugh. He said, "April like what she likes."
They all laughed and got into the car.

Deyun drove into a subdivision, they couldn't help but admire how nice the neighborhood was, upscale on the next level.

They pulled into the drive way of a two story brick house with double garage doors along with Crape myrtles and Snowball viburnums bordering the foundation.

As soon as they stepped out of the car the front door swung open. It was the first time they'd met April and from where she stood she looked like a little girl with her hair blown out.

Sarcastically Kenadi said, "What you went to Miami and cloned that girl Amara La Negra from that hip hop drama Miami show?"
But as they got closer Kenadi could see that she was a full

grown woman.
She had dark chocolate skin,
stood around five foot six and
was thicker than a master
pad lock and little bit
pregnant.

She greeted her new family
with open arms and brilliant
smile.

Kenadi said, "What's this,
aunt La'Rainne hasn't said a
word about the bun in the
oven!"

"That's because it was going
to be a surprise, we were
going to fly her up weeks
prior to the due date," replied
Deyun.

April couldnt help but notice
that Kenadi was also carry a

load.
She said, "looks like I'm not the only one and when are you due?"

"Some time in June," replied Kenadi.

It was still early and breakfast was in the making. The aroma was mouth watering. The surround sound was crisp, clean and crystal clear as "Jhene' Aiko" voice cut through the air.

As April began to set the table she said, "If you guys are hungry help yourself, there's bacon, eggs, strawberry waffles."
Krystina said, "I don't know about you but I want in," as she made her way to the sink

to wash her hands.

They all got seated and Deyun said, "Kenadi you are going to love the location of the building and around eleven we'll go check thangs out and meet up with a few people."

They ate and made conversation, before they knew it, it was almost eleven o'clock.

They pulled into a plaza off Slider Rd. which contained a dozen or so business's and immediately Kenadi knew this was the perfect location.

On the opposing sides of the building was a loan company and a glass company.

Kenadi and the contractor were introduced and quickly the two got to work designing the four hundred square foot space.

An hour later Kenadi had everything mapped out just how she wanted it, now all she had to do was sign the permits and order appliances.
The contractor estimated that it would take forty five to sixty days to finish the job with a cost around thirty thousand.

Kenadi said, "That's fine with me I'll route half to your account now to get the show on the road and Deyun im sending forty thousand to April's account so you guys can get whatever you need to get this place up and serving."

They waited while the contractor did some last minute measurements and Kenadi looked at the different color schemes, designs and logo's and she had just the person for the job, Element of Design by CHOPPTRIGG.

The color scheme she had chosen was scarlet and silver and the name of the restaurant would be Raven's Haven.

The liquor liscences were nothing to get and the menu had already been mapped out but there were still a few modifications in the process.

After signing the contract they went back to Deyuns place and did some online surfing for appliances.

Kenadi glanced at her watch not realizing that it was after one p.m. as she thought about Taven and what he was doing and why he hadn't called. She opted to call him but decided to wait til later.

Moments later her cell vibrated, she looked at the display and it was Sinneria calling to see when she would be back, she had another hundred thousand to spend.

She said, "Do you think you can five hundred of them pills I got another eight thousand for that."

"No pressure, I call you as soon as get in tomorrow."

Kenadi had gotten accustom to racking in thousands. She knew to flip the hundred thousand, make a thirty thousand dollar profit along with the extra town pounds and two kilos another sixty thousand dollar profit. She knew what the lick was and couldn't lose.

After they hung up she called Flagg.
On the third ring he answered already knowing what the lick read, she didn't have to do to much explaining all she did was relay some numbers.

Since she was pregnant he didn't want her to take any more chances than she already were so he decided to deliver it peronally and he also knew that his man Three would be very upset if he knew that she was still in the game.

Before she hung up she said, "How about a double up and I pay two hundred thousand?"

"I get it cheap, say one sixty and you keep forty," replied Flagg.

She knew the money would generate in no time and Sinneria would be calling again very soon plus she couldn't wait to get back home and recruit some one's daughter to help her with these babies and she had the perfect candidate.

Jy-Jy was the one, she was smart, mature and dependable.

Kenadi stopped momentarily rubbing her belly feeling the side effects of being pregnant as she thought about life and how good it was at the moment. Fatigue had turned into a major factor as she wasn't use to carrying the extra weight.

Around three p.m. April began gathering her things. Mondays and Wednesdays after work she and a few friends went to the shooting range.

"What kind if work are you into?" Asked Kenadi.

April laughed and said, "I teach tenth grade biology and the mayor suggests that every one should have a little training in the field just in case. Schools aren't safe like the old days but I highly doubt we'll have any threats and honestly I've grown accustom to the rush that I get, would you like to come along? It would be fun.

Kenadi was hesitant about it all but made up her mind and went along.

She thought, "Maybe I could learn a thing or two. Kenadi was already liking April.

Something about her stood out and she was clearly the one for Deyun and Kenadi was more than happy for her cousin.

Thirty minutes later they pulled into the parking lot of Hamilton's ammunition, a local shooting range and upon entering they went directly to the front desk where they produced their identification and the entrance fee.
At first Kenadi was skeptic and didn't feel comfortable, she'd shot a pistol before but wasn't fond of them but on the other band April was handled one with style and grace.

Kenadi watched her shoot a

forty caliber pistol, a two twenty three assault rifle and a sixteen gauge combat shot gun.

Kenadi was scared to death but decided to give it a try. After the third clip she had a handle of things and shot over four hundred rounds of ammunition in ten minutes.

By the time they left, Kenadi was wanting a pistol and made a vow to get one as soon as she hit Tallahassee.

Thru and thru the girls had had a good time and Kenadi decided to stay overnight and fly in first thing tomorrow.

For dinner Deyun wanted steak and shrimp but all

Kenadi had a taste for was something pickled.

While Krystina prepared the table Kenadi texted her cousin Zero about the pills.

He instantly texted back, "I Got you family."

Kenadi really had fun and totally forgot about calking Taven.

<u>Eight</u>
No. 5

Rabbi and Three boarded their flight to California and landed at the San Diego international around ten a.m.

Pomakii waited as the men got their luggage. Rabbi introduced the two.

Pomakii said, "Nice to meet you handsome. She eyed him then the wedding band and said, "I've heard a lot of good things about you and I hope we get better acquainted in the near future.

Three already knew what she had in mind and couldn't help but notice that she spoke with a Canadian accent fused with a lot of broken English.

Walking to the parking lot Taven noticed and couldn't help but admire how beautiful she really was and she wasn't your average hood rat, more like a lab rat ready to explore and experiment on any and every thing that pertained to botony and hemp.

Her petite frame was well toned giving the impression that she worked out wearing a volt yellow Mulan tee along with the matching Nike shocks and a pair of stretch pants.

Her bronze skin tone was gave her that glow like a brand new penny and her hair was styled just below her ears in a Bob giving her this amazing distinctive look not to add that she was pair toed which added on to her sex appeal.

The cocaine white Dodge Magnum came to life as the engine turned over be the trunk popped open

Rabbi and Pomakii had met six years prior at Oregon university and had become very close friends over the years. She did her thing in Botony and while he did pharmecuiticles.

Pomakii worked for a medical marijuana grower and supplier called Gauranteed Canibus where she experimented with different type of buds and grew some of the best essential known to man.

Over time she created her own strand called "Canadian Fantana" which was a form of hydroponics.

Thirty minutes later Pomakii served into the parking lot of a warehouse like building.

Upon entering they went through security and down a long hall that consisted of doors with numbers above them.

Pomakii pulled out a card and slid it through the slot and the door instantly popped open.

Taven took in the scenery and noticed aquariums, marijuana trees that stood six feet tall and the aroma of cultivated buds. Hesaid, "Damn this is one luxurius warehouse."

"Do you live here?"

"As a matter of a fact I do but I have and apartment also even though I spend eighty percent of my time here plus Iguadola my iguana gets monkey when I'm away to long."

Back home in Florida Three had seen a million lizards but not as big as this one.

As Rabbi and Pomakii made conversation Three observed and listened.
Pomakii told the two to get comfortable and that they had nothing to worry about, everything that went on in Guaranteed Cannabis was legal.

Taven inhaled then exhaled the exotic stinch that hung in the air, to many to tell the difference.

Taven said, "I'm thinking about starting my own strand, what would it take and cost?"

"With the proper soil, proper lighting and ventilation it want be nothing to it just waiting for the plant to develops and hope that it something different."

Pomakii broke it all down to him then turned on the halogen led lights that light up the enormous room.

She then began talking business, about the celebrities she'd worked with such as Willie Nelson, Seth Rogan, Jonah Hill, Owen Wilson, Chris tucker and Woody Harrelson. She also showed him forty two small plants of some killer herb that Kendrick Lamar concocted called CompCago which was a hybrid between Purple Haze and Bleu Dream. Her next question was one he thought she'd never ask.

She said, "Do you smoke?"

"Do I, like a freight train," replied Taven.

She left momentarily and came back with a vaporizer that worked by pumping THC fumes in evasive clouds that polluted the air.

Pomakii walked to a large glass cabinet that contaned small jars full of popcorn shaped buds.

"Pick one," she replied as she signaled for Taven to come where she was.

He looked over the different types of green reading the label's not realizing that there was this many different kind of strands like Blackberry banana hydro, and Kumquat Kush which he quickly retrieve from the shelf.

Pomakii put a gram in the vaprorizer and gave a gram to Rabbi along with a cigarello to roll up.

Rabbi wasted no time as he rolled the marijuana up where he light up on a buns in burner that had a mason jar at contained a clear liquid that wouldn't boil.

Rabbi toked the blunt and coughed before passing it Taven who toked it lightly searching for a taste. As he passed it to Pomakii he said, "What's that in the Mason jar?"

"One hundred percent THC, its being evaporated a little bit over twenty five percent of this stuff give you couch lock."

"Explain," replied Taven.

"They medically prescribe it for a number of things and Couch lock, well you'll find out in a little while," she replied with a devilish grin.

Twenty minutes Taven was stuck to the couch as he watched Rabbi play Madden on Wii. The eighty inch screen glistened and under the black light the Bob Marley poster gave off psychedelic feel as he tried to focus.

He and Pomakii caught eye contact. She smiled and said, "Blowing on that Bruce Leroy will knock that dick in the dirt. Y'all hungry?"

"We can order or trust in my youth."

"And what would that be?" Asked Taven.

Pomaki pointed into the small kitchen area where there were shelves that contained each and every box of cereal known to man.

Taven looked at Rabbi and said, "I would love some of

them flakes but I need me a
number five, where the
Captain D's at.

<u>Nine</u>
Almost Don't Count

 T wo days had passed and the research Nazara had done on the cripple homicide was really paying off. She had obtained the names of the two men I evolved in the murder now all she had to do was locate them.
The two men were brothers from the North Atlanta area. According to the report the two men own a few local laundry mat that they used as drop off's.

People came in with baskets of laundry, the usual uniting suspicious about that but it under the laundry there were kilo's, a perfect location for for doing drop's. A quick swap in broad day undetected and this has been going on for years but his last drop didn't gonas planned and you know it couldn't be but one of two things. Drug's' money or both.
Now we are waiting on the identity on the three men that were found in the corner of Palmetto ave.

While she scanned her notes Detective Jackson called the Sheriff Sadirolf.

Sadirolf said, "Talk to me, anything new?
Our best is ready to work this case all you have to do is tell me where to start."

"As of now we have reason to believe that the two are in South America and we are investigating a safe house in Rhode Island. We now have a drug bust that occured in Miami that I believe is going to be very vital and may help this investigation.
Trust me I'll update you if anything comes about."

While the two men talked the identity of the men hit the fax machine.

Nazara read over the the papers but none of the names nor the faces looked familiar. Jackson hung up the phone and she handed him the paper work. He recognized all the names and Nazira quickly came to a conclusion. She said, "I bet they are all networking, all three if them are from different locations."

"Its like they met up did the drop with Garland brothers, and something didn't add up there's a shoot out and know we have three dead men.

Nazira pulled their records while Jackson studied while Jackson matched faces with names, something rung a bell he just couldn't pin point what was at the moment.

<u>Ten</u>
The Program

*K*enadi and Krystina made it back to Tallahassee and was glad to have their feet back on solid ground. Kenadi drove her mother home and contacted her cousin Zero about the pills then Flagg, it was time to get this money.

Thirty minutes later Zero pulled into the drive way with the pills. She got in and they made the transaction.

Before she got out she said, "I'll probably need a thousand next to time!"

"No problem you know I got you covered," replied Zero as he pulled pulled out of the drive way.

Before Kenadi could her through the door good with the pills blue led light lit up the the front of the condo as the cream colored Land Rover Discovery drove up.

After a moment of blindness from the light she realized it was Flagg.

 He parked and got out carrying two black duffle bags and as he aproached the front door she told him to come in leading him through the living room where he waited.

The orange and white Harley Davidson truck blended in as Peligro sat patiently watching on the right moment to kill again.

Kenadi went up stairs to get the money and by the time she came back down Flagg had the product layed out.

She inspected the product while he thumbed through the bills just before placing them inside of the duffle bags grabbing them by the straps he told Kenadi to call whenever she was ready to re-up."

She said, "Look for a call in about two weeksm your boy will be calling soon, I know

he has a trick up his sleeve."
Flagg smiled and said, "I'll be
waiting.

 Kenadi locked the front door
then armed the alarm
symstem.
She then relocated the drug
to her closet.

She'd seen enough drug
related movies to know and
taught her self how to cut the
drugs and she was area
corners away from cutting
the product.

The kilo's were pre wrapped
to perfection. She damn near
had to use a hacksaw to get
the package, breaking them
down putting them on the
scale Kenadi measured the
thousand in grams splitting

the brick replacing the other half with backing soda using a blended to mix the the two.

Afterwards she resealed the product for distribution. Kenadi then examined the marijuana as she inhaled then exhaled the exotic aroma if the buds.

She then serperated the product putting it in the safe until time for distribution.

Just as she closed the safe the house alarm went off startling her.

Kenadi instantly went into guard mode as she tip toed through the house looking for a sign of an intruder but after scaling every square inch of

the enormous condo she came up with nothing thinking that it was just a precautions glitch.
Seven minutes later there were police cruisers surrounding the condo responding to the alarm. Little did she know Peligro was still on the job tryning to complete his mission, but his timing didn't match up to making every attempt seem impossible.

The following morning Kenadi texted Sinneria telling her that the water was fine, meaning that everything was a go.

Sinneria texted back, "See you around five."

Shortly after Kenadi texted Taven who instantly returned her call.

She said, "Bae what's up, how is things coning along?"

"Honestly things are going as planned, I'm still trying to decide on this strand and we are meeting with the executives over Biotic Botony and hopefully things will work out."
"Where are you at this moment?"

"We've made it back to Tally and now I'm waiting on aunt La'Rainne to show her face, she's hasn't been to the house since I we left and I'm stating to worry cause this is really unlike her but little did

Kenadi know Peligro had some how slid into the condo undetected and kidnapped and murdered her aunt and that was just the begining of the devil once again doing his thing.

Kenadi shook the thought again and began to explain the status of their soon to be restaurant in Kentucky anbd the doctors appointment that she had at two o'clock. She assured him that she would call him and update him on the status of his babies and they hung up.

Thanksgiving was two weeks away and little did they know a small dosage of hell would be raised in between then and January.

To be continued...

Thank you family and friends
I hope you all enjoyed 90°
The Lick, the begining of a
disasterous success and stay
tuned there's more and see
how this plays out.

Author La'mar Donald

Follow me:
FB@author La'mar Donald

Cover design:
FB@Element of Design by CHOPPTRIGG

www.ingramcontent.com/pod-product-compliance
Lightning Source LLC
Chambersburg PA
CBHW022008170726
47994CB00023B/2427